# MORE PRAISE FOR GOD LOVES HAIR:

"A book for all ages, this will be especially welcomed by contemporary genderqueer youth and twenty somethings, who will see themselves in these vividly realized pages." —Booklist (starred review)

"A rich and powerful exploration of gender, sexuality, religion, race, and the desire to fit in." —Quill & Quire (starred review)

"Shraya's stripped-down prose has documentary force, and Neufeld's illustrations, with their intersecting planes of translucent color and their linoleum block-style images, add humor and bite. It's an important addition to the library of coming-out literature." —Publishers Weekly (starred review)

"Running the emotional spectrum from shame to pleasure and acceptance, Shraya offers a refreshing window into the intimate struggles of youth." —Kirkus Reviews

# GOD LOVES HAIR

TENTH ANNIVERSARY EDITION

**Vivek Shraya**

**Foreword by Cherie Dimaline**

Illustrations by Juliana Neufeld

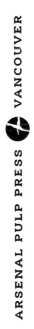

ARSENAL PULP PRESS · VANCOUVER

ARSENAL PULP PRESS
Suite 202–211 East Georgia St.
Vancouver, BC V6A 1Z6
Canada
*arsenalpulp.com*

The publisher gratefully acknowledges the support of the Canada Council for the Arts and the British Columbia Arts Council for its publishing program, and the Government of Canada, and the Government of British Columbia (through the Book Publishing Tax Credit Program), for its publishing activities.

Arsenal Pulp Press acknowledges the xʷməθkʷəy̓əm (Musqueam), Sḵwx̱wú7mesh (Squamish), and səl̓ilwətaʔɬ (Tsleil-Waututh) Nations, custodians of the traditional, ancestral, and unceded territories where our office is located. We pay respect to their histories, traditions, and continuous living cultures and commit to accountability, respectful relations, and friendship.

Edited by Katherine Friesen and Maureen Hynes
Original book design by Michelle Campos Castillo

Printed and bound in Canada

Library and Archives Canada Cataloguing in Publication
Title: God loves hair / Vivek Shraya ; foreword by Cherie Dimaline ; illustrations by Juliana Neufeld.
Names: Shraya, Vivek, 1981– author. | Dimaline, Cherie, 1975– writer of foreword. | Neufeld, Juliana, 1982– illustrator.
Description: Tenth anniversary edition | Short stories.
Identifiers: Canadiana (print) 20200210254 | Canadiana (ebook) 20200210343 | ISBN 9781551528137 (hardcover) | ISBN 9781551528144 (HTML).
Classification: LCC PS8637.H73 G63 2020 | DDC jC813/.6—dc23

For the boy who was almost lost.

# CONTENTS

# FOREWORD

It has been ten years since Vivek Shraya published her groundbreaking and innovative book God Loves Hair. It is as relevant, necessary, and remarkable now as it was when she first refused refusal and ensured other brown, queer, struggling kids would find a home in these pages.

Filling the curves of every letter in each word after carefully curated word, Shraya manages to give us the entirety of her early universe in the succinct poetic language that has cemented her place in our literary landscape, a place that enjoys the full view afforded to those who have climbed to the top. In fact, she has gone beyond us, but as is her way, she waits patiently for us to catch up, beckoning us to follow along a path only she can discern but from which it is impossible to wander. I can hear her aunties' bangles and smell her mother's perfume as she waves us on.

God Loves Hair is the book every child should know exists, that every person should read—but not too fast, though that compulsion is almost impossible to resist. It is one of those rare offerings that circles many issues—from bullying to shame, self-preservation to family history—all from inside the very eye of the storm that is adolescence.

Reading God Loves Hair is a gift that challenges as it soothes, bringing the two extremes to the reader within the rhythm of a hymn. Both Shraya's generous style and sharp precision are captured in every note, in each line.

They say loving yourself is an act of rebellion, so then the small, beautiful stories in this collection become a manifesto to that movement—self-love at all costs, under any weight. From the pleasant ache of the minute change found in tweezing to the shattering, deep understanding discoverable in the earthly presence of God, this book takes us through the expansive geography of devotion to an ever-growing self.

God is my first love.

God is my first best friend.

God is my first broken heart.

Only a unique and powerful voice, speaking from the depth of watching ancestors, can lead us through beauty while paying equal mind to the shadows it casts. We are awestruck by the young protagonist's close relationship with a higher power, and at the same time bear witness while he changes after gym class, making his body as small as he can in the corner of the locker room. We ache to feel the kind of peace that descends when the AUM unravels on Sundays like a dropped spool of ribbon, and quake at the burn and tightness of being physically attacked in school hallways.

How can such extremes coexist in one life? And how could they possibly quiet down long enough for Shraya to hear the words that would hold them? This is the magic of Vivek Shraya. She has found a way to hold all the antithetical facets of life in the simple geometry of letters made into words, then crafted into stories that sing and weep and honour and celebrate, all at the same time. And then she goes even further, enabling us to join her in the songs made equally of mourning and defiance. Even if she is, always, just a little bit ahead of us. After all, isn't that the job of a storyteller, of a true artist? To break the ground and smooth the path so that, no matter how many shadows fall in the way, we are always aware of the beauty, the achingly generous and enormously powerful beauty, just up ahead.

Vivek, I would follow you anywhere. Chi miigwetch for singing us home, every single time.

CHERIE DIMALINE
December 9, 2019

# PREFACE

Art has been my greatest teacher. Although my work is frequently categorized as being "about identity" (as opposed to work by non-brown, non-queer artists, which is ... "identity free"), often the opposite is true: the art I make shapes, and even creates, my identity. This is especially true of *God Loves Hair*. Back when I first self-published the book in 2010, I identified as male. I dedicated the book to "the boy who was almost lost." Some readers have generously interpreted the book as a trans narrative, but when I wrote it, I had no idea that it was a ship sailing me towards Transgender Island. The art was ahead of me. It's almost like I felt that I could convey something about myself on the page before I could express it as a being.

Similarly, my foray into books was actually intended to be a one-off. Writing God Loves Hair was a coping strategy when I was heartbroken by the static state of my music career. The joke my friends tell about God Loves Hair is that I wrote a few lines in my closet (literally—my closet did double duty as my office) and "came out," announcing: "I've written a book!" The audacity of this declaration was amusing coming from someone with no formal experience as a writer, and with no prior ambitions of being a writer. But the process of writing the book, and then reading from it across North America and India, revealed to me that my voice could do more than sing—it could tell stories.

Looking back, I have so much admiration for my twenty-eight-year-old self, for the way he channelled his grief, driving full throttle into the unknown, into something new. For taking a creative risk. May I always have this courage.

The innocence of creating "the first" in any medium is precious. When I wrote *God Loves Hair*, I wasn't dreaming of lists, of awards, of being picked by Heather. I didn't know what the barometers of success were. Consequently, I wrote from a place of wonder, free from the constraints of the pop song format, free from industry or audience pressure. Perhaps this is why when I read *God Loves Hair* now, there is very little I would change, almost nothing I regret—unlike a lot of the art I have made. Perhaps this is why I find myself jumping from medium to medium, perpetually trying to re-create the elusive innocence of that first.

After chasing a record deal for most of my twenties, I felt my agency was restored by self-publishing two editions of *God Loves Hair* (2010 and 2012). I learned that I didn't need the support of an institution to connect with audiences. Instead, I became my own institution. I learned first-hand how to be a publisher, a publicist, and a booking agent. This experience was invaluable when Arsenal Pulp Press published the third edition of the book, in 2014—not only because I did not expect to simply hand off the book to a publisher who would then do all the heavy lifting, but also because I was now able to enter a relationship with an institution with an understanding of my own value. Instead of being an overly demanding or subservient novice, I could work with my publisher as a team.

Although the book's dedication remains unchanged (I'm a purist), I find myself thinking about who else has been almost lost. In the past ten years writers Leslie Feinberg and Toni Morrison, and actress Sridevi, have died—but their legacies radiate. Feinberg's *Stone Butch Blues* and Morrison's *The Bluest Eye* were the two books that inspired me to write this one, which features a story inspired by and named after Sridevi. I am grateful to these humans, who ensured that the girl in me was not lost either.

VIVEK SHRAYA
August 30, 2019

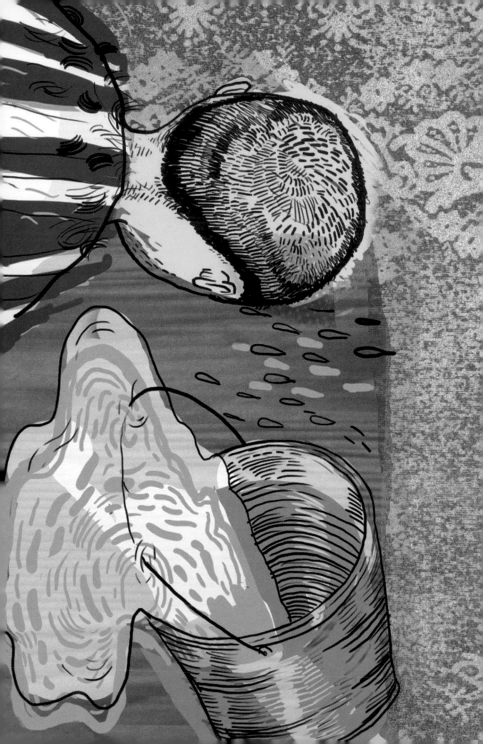

# GOD LOVES HAIR

My mother grows up in a big house in Ceylon with wide balconies and open windows. Her mother tells her that she is the sunlight. She is loved.

But she is a girl.

From the instant a girl is born, her parents worry. *How will we keep her safe? How will we make sure that she is educated enough, worthy enough for a husband? How will we afford to pay for her wedding, her dowry?* My mother is part of a collective of four daughters, each one representing a series of burdens. She has a brother too, but his presence in the home is light or at least one the family is happy to bear and even display proudly. He is his parents' greatest achievement, the assurance that the family name will live on. No one worries about him. *He is a man, he can stand on his own two feet.*

My mom does her best to lessen her weight, combing the knots out of her younger sister's hair, fetching water from the well. Her fluency in French and actress-like beauty also guarantee that she won't have too much trouble receiving a proposal from a doctor, engineer, or lawyer when she's ready. But when her father unexpectedly dies, every day that she and her sisters remain unwed is another day their mom, now a single parent of five, spends in distress. The pressure is on my mother and marry wise is replaced by marry fast. She finds that she is no longer as attractive to potential suitors because the absence of a father suggests the absence of a dowry. You should have just married the neurosurgeon who came to see you last month. He was from a rich family, he would have been good to you. Then I would have one less daughter to worry about. She silently promises to herself that she will marry the next suitor who knocks on her door. The lucky beneficiary of this promise is the man from Canada with the thick sideburns, the multicoloured tie, and only a Master's degree. My dad. They meet, are engaged, and then married in the span of ten days.

When the time comes to have children of her own, my mother is unwavering about her desire to have sons. Two healthy sons. So she does what any determined Hindu would do: she barters with God. If You grant me two healthy sons, I vow to give them their first haircuts at the Temple of Seven Hills in Tirupathi, India. It is believed that the hair on your head is what makes you beautiful. Shaving it off pleases God because it means you have chosen Him over your appearance.

My mother is pregnant. I am a basketball. As her tiny body expands, her prayers intensify. Let him be a boy. Let him look just like his father. Let him live. Every other firstborn in her family has died through miscarriage or stillbirth. She is comforted every time I kick.

I am born the day after Valentine's Day. My mother examines me closely. I have a penis. No missing toe or spare finger. She is overjoyed and cries: *God is great!* Like most Indian babies, I have a full head of jet-black hair. It grows fast and long, testing my mom's resolve. But true to her word, no scissors or razor come near my head. My parents decide it would be best for their wallet if they try to make another baby boy right away. This would save them from having to go to India twice to fulfill my mother's end of the bargain. In the interim, my hair is managed into several mini-pigtails and eventually into one long, thin ponytail.

My, what a cute baby girl you have! Your daughter is so pretty! How old is she? She looks just like her dad. What's her name? She has such chubby cheeks!

My first haircut is in Tirupathi, next to my baby brother, just as my mother prophesized. I cry as the barber pours warm water over my newly shaven head, the small cuts, made by his severe grip and his old razor, burning. God is happy. I am two years old.

# BED HUMPER

*Say your prayers. I dread this moment. Having to look up at the creased picture, ripped from an old calendar, hanging on my wall. He sees me.*

It's Lord Venkateshwara. He is the Scary God, faceless except for his teeth, who steals your hair if you are bad. I whisper a sloka and then climb into bed, turning my face to the opposite wall.

I listen for silence. When it's safe, I roll onto my stomach, squeeze my worn-out baby blanket, and quietly push my body up and down against the bed.

The next morning, I touch my head. Hair still there. I know it's wrong. No one has told me so, but I know it is. It has to be. It feels good. I don't even know what it's called, but I know it's wrong. One day when my brother walks in on me, I tell him I am exercising.

I know that if I want something from God, I will have to forsake "it." Dear God, if I get a Ninja Turtle blimp for Christmas, I promise not to do "it" for three weeks. I break my promise. Soon after, a night exercise ends in what feels like a short burst of pee but almost from a different place. My hands are tingling. I turn on my night lamp for a closer look down there. White goop. I broke it! God is punishing me!

I seek comfort from my mom. She is sitting on her bed, sewing a button onto her sweater. I stand by the door.

Moooom, I have a proooobiem... The other day ... um ... I ... woke up ... and there was this white liquid coming out of my private part. Is that normal?

She looks at me. I step back.

Yes. That's normal.

I pause and then turn around before she changes her mind.

# LIPSTICK

The sky is a promising blue but the empty house is all mine. My mother and her younger sister are drinking chai on the front porch. My five-year-old mind races through all my favourite things to do, deciding how best to use this extraordinary time and space. I think about eating the Play-Doh kept in the craft corner of the basement or maybe sucking the vanilla pudding out of the tin cups that I am not strong enough to fully open. Then I picture my mother's makeup case.

It is unguarded!

This is my chance to know her secrets, access her powers. I rush up the stairs, almost tripping into her washroom, and tear open her magic kit. I am blinded. All the bright colours are dazzling. But I am greedy for the colours that hide, the glossy surprises caged within lipstick shells. They call to me. One by one, I remove their lids, twist the blushing sticks to the top, smear my face like oil on canvas. Then I smash the lids back on, completely crushing the lipsticks.

My mother and aunt come inside to find lipstick casualties strewn across the washroom floor and my stained face, beaming and proud. My aunt spanks me until I am blue in the bum. Some of the lipsticks were hers.

# DRESS UP

My brother and I live in a Lego world, building amusement out of unsuspecting materials. Couch pillows become forts, quilts become flower-patterned wings, and his headboard becomes a stage for puppet shows. We have also discovered a secret cave under his bed, perfect for hiding in, which is particularly useful when mom yells from downstairs: Fold the laundry! But the change I love most happens when we play dress up. We wear each other's clothes. His are smaller and tighter than my own. I like the feeling of the fabric choking my body. It's like being touched all over.

I like dressing up at school too. Whenever there is a school play, I beg for the girl roles. Girls get to have long, flowing hair, some days French-braided, other days curled. They get to show off shiny earrings and delicate bracelets. And girls get to wear actual colours. Like popsicle pink and poppy red. Why should they have all the fun? It's pretty easy convincing everyone that it would be funnier for a boy to play a girl, my pre-pubescent high-pitched voice an asset, but secretly I just want the chance to put on my mother's velvet emerald-coloured dress. It too is small and tight, with a life of its own. I step into the dress and close my eyes. I let her Estée Lauder scent envelop me and feel her like a current of electricity, both warm and fierce. I become her. I am beautiful.

When we travel to India to visit my parent's family, my aunts tell me how pretty I am. I seize the opportunity to test out their observations. Maybe you should dress me up in a sari and see what I would look like as a girl, I say coyly. They jump at the chance. They spread out their rainbow sari collections on the bed, and I feel like a princess as I choose the bold magenta and black one. It looks like something my mom would wear. They spin me around in the endless sheer fabric that smells like oil and mothballs and pleat it a couple times at the front so it looks like an accordion hanging from my waist. But my transformation isn't complete. Bangles all the way up to my elbows, thick black eyeliner, a string of white jasmine flowers in my hair. From afar, my dad thinks I am some sweet village girl. I am the prettiest little girl in the world.

# SRIDEVI

Have you ever played MASH? Just a pen and paper can tell you what kind of home you will have (M for Mansion, A for Apartment, S for Shack, and H for house), what car you'll drive, what city you'll live in, and which girl you will marry. Sridevi, the famous Bollywood actress, is always on the top of my list of dream wives. No one can dance or act like her. She is a true star.

She might not be the best singer, as she painfully showcased in Chandni, but that's why they typically use playback singers in Bollywood, which is just a fancy way of saying the actors lipsynch. And no one is as beautiful as her. Not my dad's childhood crush, Hema Malini, and certainly not this new young hot-shot in town everyone is raving about, Madhuri Dixit. People are so fickle.

My favourite Sridevi movie of all time is Nagina, where she plays a woman who is the human incarnation of a snake, except she doesn't know it. When she hears the snake charmer's nasal song, she faints onto her bed. Her innocent brown eyes turn a menacing blue as she starts convulsing to the sound, completely entranced and powerless. She puts on a white sari, adorns herself with diamond jewellery, and then confronts the snake charmer through glorious choreography.

I like pretending that somewhere deep down inside, I too am a snake, just like her, waiting to be set free. I pull the thin yellow sheet off my bed, wrap it around my head, and twist and twist it as though I have a long Sridevi-esque braid. I turn on the *Nagina* soundtrack and make my eyes really really big. My hips slowly begin to wind as I struggle against the music. *Main teri dushman, dushman tu mera, main naagin tu sapheraa.* Then, when the ache in my stomach becomes unbearable, I let go and dance.

# PERVERT

It's always been just the four of us. My dad, my mom, my brother, and me. No extended family at Christmas or Thanksgiving. No favourite aunties or uncles.

My grandmother, Ajji, once visited from India, bringing with her a treasure chest of stories about my mom, a passage into a world I had never known; apparently my mom was my age once. But when Ajji got homesick, she accused my parents of trying to kill her. My parents don't have any real friends either. The ones they do have, the ones they call upon only in an emergency, they pay back with gifts or repeatedly invite for dinner until my mother is satisfied that our silent debt has been paid off. I too seldom have my friends over, but if I do, they will also receive a hearty meal. In no one we trust, and the house is our fortress.

My dad shares his birthday with his older brother, also known as The Doctor, The Actor, The Favourite. They never speak, except for on that day. When I am seven years old, my uncle and his Golden Family decide to visit us from the United States of America. There is a lot of talk about how attractive my cousins Anish and Praveen are. Praveen is fair and has light eyes. The more a brown person looks like a white person, the more attention they seem to get. Even if they are ugly. But I am preoccupied with the idea of an extended family, having a family that extends past the four of us, and that there is an actual resemblance among all of us. I see my giant nose on their faces. We are related! I imagine Anish and Praveen are the older brothers I never had, and I love them immediately, desperately.

One evening, Anish is on the living room couch watching the Stanley Cup playoffs. I am on the floor by his feet focusing hard on the TV screen, hoping this interest will impress him. But his own focus on the game is unshakeable. I turn around, wind my arm under his knee, and make my hand the shape of a snake in between his legs, in honour of my favourite Bollywood film Nagira, trying to get his attention. Look! I hiss proudly. Anish looks at me and my snake hand, his eyes groaning, then looks to his brother on the opposite couch and says: What a perv!

# DEAR VISHNU

They say Your skin is blue because You are infinite like the sky and the ocean of milk You rest on. I wish my skin was blue. Brown is boring, it blends into the dirt or concrete background. So I draw on my hands and arms with a blue ink pen. My teacher says that I can get ink poisoning, but this only inspires me to draw more for I have heard that it was drinking poison that turned Lord Shiva's skin dark blue.

I want to be a modern version of You. I would wear a peacock feather in my hair like You, maybe use my mom's curling iron to match Your wavy locks, and get my ears pierced. But my four arms would carry a walkman, a book, a candle, and an apple. There should be a "Take Your Believer to Work Day" so I can study You in action, ask questions, and take notes. I am jealous of Goddess Lakshmi, Your consort, for the eternity she gets to spend by Your side. Does she know how lucky she is? If You smile, she shares it. If You speak, she hears it. It's not fair that only one can be so close.

When my mom prays, she becomes stiff as though one wrong gesture could displease You and result in her losing her job, or worse, having to be reborn. I wish she knew the version of You that I know, the one whose adventures and victories I read about in my Amar Chitra Katha comic books. You are The Protector, the one that the demigods rush to in times of crisis. They are instantly soothed by the sight of You, decorated with flowers and gold, and Your compassionate counsel. Countless evil demons are slayed by Your mighty chakra or bow and arrow, but You always appear calm, never angry, as though even destruction is an act of love. How do You do it? Sometimes there is a fire in me, and when it comes out, it's never as pretty.

Maybe it's the blue that keeps You cool. If only I were blue.

# GIRLS ARE MOTHERS AND SISTERS

Men sit on the left side and women on the right. We are divided by a red carpet. This is "to keep the monkey mind from being distracted." Whoever thought up this tradition must have had a lot of foresight as most of my friends are girls, and we would definitely end up chatting during meditation if we were allowed to sit together.

I learn at Sunday school that girls are like my mother or my sisters and need to be treated as such. I have always wanted a sister, someone's hair to braid or nails to paint, so this is really a blessing. I can tell my own mother is pleased with my staunch adherence to this rule, the way I don't notice girls outside of sisterhood. The way I don't notice that my mother's latest craft course creation, a ceramic statue of a woman that she calls The Nude, is actually naked. I am puzzled by this choice of name when clearly the statue is covered in gold paint. But I curb my curiosity after seeing how horrified my parents are when one of our houseguests keeps accidentally bumping into The Nude. *Did you see how Gopal was looking at The Nude? He couldn't take his eyes off it!*

Note to self: Don't stare at The Nude.

The older I get, and the older my "sisters" get, the harder it is not to notice the mountains of physical differences between us. *Breasts.* Breasts are beginning to poke out everywhere. At the Centre, sculptures of goddesses that once appeared to me as inanimate depictions are suddenly alive, boasting their large bare breasts. She is my mother! I train myself never to look in that direction, and if my eyes wander in curiosity or by accident, I immediately whisper Sai Ram, the name of God, for forgiveness.

Going to Walmart with my parents is the ultimate test. We always end up having to cut through the women's underwear section. I focus my attention on the ground, making a melody out of the tile patterns, and walk as fast as I can to avoid potential sin. Sai Ram, Sa Ram, Sai Ram.

# ES EE EX

Four o'clock is The Young and the Restless time. It's the daycare owner's favourite TV show. I like it because the women are stylish and confident, and the men are handsome and wear suits. Sometimes they take off their shirts to the sound of saxophone music and hold each other tightly. But it's different than how my mom hugs me. It's prolonged and almost devotional, with their hands moving all over each other. I imagine what that holding would feel like. That holding is called S.E.X.

My parents don't like S.E.X. Anytime we watch a movie together and it looks like S.E.X. might happen, they frantically fumble with the fast-forward, only to fast-forward most of the movie away. Or they just hold the couch pillows over my face. They think Full House, the family sitcom featuring the baby Olsen twins, is for grownups. And whenever my dad tries to kiss my mom, she always pulls back and gets this look on her face like she might need to go to the washroom. Doooonn'tt!

So why have my parents signed my Grade Five S.E.X. education permission form?

The video we are shown is nothing like The Young and the Restless. No candlelight, no bubble bath, no lace. Just a strict-looking man in a lab coat talking about dreams that make boys wet their pants. Blood floods inside girls. How to put a "condom" on a banana. What is this? I squirm in my seat and wish I had my own remote control to fast-forward past the nudity. I glance at my teacher's face, hoping she looks as uncomfortable as I am, a sign that this viewing wasn't her idea. She looks bored. The video ends. No holding.

At daycare, I rant to the other kids: They were talking about S.E.X! ESS EEE EEX! Do you even know what that is?? How could they show us those things, those bad things? Polluting our minds at school! They were even showing us pictures of boobies! How could they embarrass the girls like that! I just wanted to go up to the projector and TURN IT OFF!

I rant in the car, all the way home. I think my parents are proud.

# THE COLOUR PURPLE

I love when colours join forces. The smell of wax and invincible possibilities when opening a new box of crayons. Or rainbows. Like my Smurfs rainbow belt and neon rainbow suspenders. But if I had to choose just one, okay, two, then I would say yellow is my favourite colour and purple is my favourite colour to wear. My mom tells me I am "a winter" which apparently means I look good in dark "winter" colours like black (not white), navy blue, and purple. To me, purple is more "spring," like lilacs or the flavour of grapes.

I plead with my parents for a Starter baseball hat in the same way I pleaded for a New Kids on the Block sweatshirt—until they relent. I am clueless about baseball and don't really understand the point of sports. A ball being hit or thrown or kicked around doesn't captivate me the way Nancy Drew books do. But all the other boys in my class have these hats. This cluelessness proves to be critical as my parents and I are standing in front of rows and rows of hats at the store. I am dizzy from the options and the fear of buying the hat of an unpopular team. After what feels like an hour of torturous indecision, I lean on my aesthetic sensibility, and reach for the purple Los Angeles Lakers hat. I have no idea who the L.A. Lakers are or if they are any good, but at least the hat looks nice. I place it on my head. It feels too big even though my mom adjusted the strap in the back. The three of us look at my reflection in the store mirror.

I am one of the boys now.

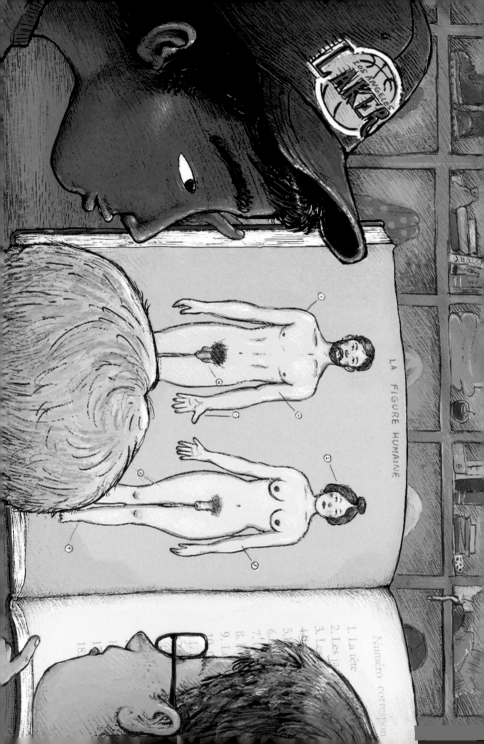

# GARDEN HOSE

When Monsieur Lambert isn't looking, the four of us boys sneak to the back of the classroom, where the thick, blue French dictionaries are piled in the corner. We snicker and quickly flip to that page, the page we come back to over and over again, the page that distracts us when we are supposed to be memorizing our times tables.

On that page is a painting of a naked, pink-skinned man and woman, side by side. Each of their body parts is labelled with a number that matches the appropriate French name, typed beside the image. But we don't see numbers or words. We are even indifferent to the man's penis, though the busy patch of hair surrounding it is a little startling. We are solely fixated on what hangs between her legs.

She has a penis, too. But hers has a giant hole at the end.

It looks like a garden hose!

Yeah, it does!

Don't you know that's how babies are made?

Reeeeaaally? How?

*The man's hose goes inside the woman's hose!*

A few years later, Nevin and I are studying the *Playboy* magazine he stole from his older brother while we wait for the bus. The women in the photographs are smiling attentively, and their legs are stretched wide. But none of them has a hose! In fact, there isn't anything dangling between their legs! Instead, they each have a pink, fleshy, mouth-like opening, yawning.

Maybe women's private parts look different in different countries.

# GIRLS ARE DANGEROUS

My dad and I are looking out at the chaos of students ahead. This is no Mill Woods Elementary. I am wearing my brand-new sneakers from Kmart, my hair is neatly combed with Amla oil, and my knapsack is stuffed with school supplies, pencils, and duo-tangs all individually labelled with my name. But I am not ready.

There is an awkward silence in the car. I am not sure what feels more foreign, my new timetable and its listing of new room numbers and new teacher last names or sharing a first with my dad. I tell myself this is what bonding feels like.

Finally, he turns to me, and I am sure he is going to wish me luck or tell me to study hard, something to inspire me to greatness on my first day of Junior High.

He says: *Stay away from girls. They are dangerous.*

# GAYLORD!

Junior High has marked the sudden death of sweat pants. They have been replaced by name-brand denim and name calling which will continue every day for the next six years.

Blond-haired, blue-eyed Will Jenson walks close behind me on my way to class. He is on his tippy toes as though he is wearing high heels, fluttering his hands, and talking with a lisp to his audience of jocks. Is that what I look like? Do you have to be such a sissy? They laugh, and I pretend I am oblivious. They have to laugh because Will is the most popular boy in school. Maybe if I laughed too, Will and I could be friends. He kicks me and I say, Sorry. He is puzzled. He kicks me again, this time timidly, like a child unsure of his own strength, and I apologize again. His friends find this funny. So he keeps kicking, they keep laughing, and I keep apologizing. I am bound to sorry, as though it's my only defense, as though each sorry holds a tiny spark of dignity.

The same jocks surround me by my locker later and warn me of impending dangers. Are you sure no one has beaten you up? You are definitely going to get beat up in high school. Definitely. One of the brown jocks, the one who laughs the loudest, follows me into the washroom. He stands wide at the stall right next to me, making his presence known. I pee as fast as I can, focusing my eyes straight down, thinking about how our matching skin doesn't protect me and how that feels like a betrayal.

I look for safety with the girls. We have more in common, like our love for Jodeci and General Hospital. I am safe for them too. I am the boy they can talk to about their crushes on the other boys. Maybe I am too safe. Mia Zinner, one of my few friends, likes to tell me how much she wishes I was dead. It's only 9:30 a.m. but I just want to kill you, Gaylord.

When I ask my parents if I can change schools, my dad tells me that my hairstyle is the real problem. In India, boys who part their hair like yours, in the middle, are ... you know ...

So I learn which hallways to avoid (Sissy!) and which faces to avoid (If you ever look at me again, I will pound the shit out of you, you fucking fag). How to walk a little firmer, talk a little deeper, be a little smaller. But I can't make it stop.

I catch an episode of *The Wonder Years* when Kevin is getting picked on by a bully. *Loser! Loser! Loser!* Fed up one day, Kevin responds, *Fine! I am a loser!* The bully responds, *You are??* in shock. He never picks on Kevin again. I immediately take note and am determined to test it out the next day:

*Gaylord!!*

*Fine! I am a Gaylord!*

*You are??* (Bingo! Just as predicted!)

*Yes! Yes, I am!*

*Do you even know what that means?*

Um. Sure I do. It means ...loser ...?

No! It means you like boys!

# BUBBLE BUTT

We are junior scientists with our microscopes. We discover what mitosis and meiosis look like under the lens. But the real focus is always on each other, specifically each other's body parts: Krissy Bell's huge breasts, Zack Mason's huge biceps, Travis Reeves' supposedly small penis. And Mr Mitchell's bum.

Mr Mitchell is my gym teacher and he is perfect. His polo shirts stretch over his heroic shoulders and chest as though they were tailored for his body alone. All the women teachers seem to smile just a little bigger when he talks to them. Even his supposed flaws are attractive, like the way his forehead shines where his sandy hair has begun to recede. But his real gift is behind him.

I have never really paid attention to any bum before, but Mr Mitchell's is hard to ignore, especially in the tight blue jeans he wears. It is magnetic. Juicy even. Just the right amount of lift and bounce. Lisa Tober calls it (and him) "Bubble Butt."

This fascination with my gym teacher's bum has led to an intense curiosity about what kind of underwear he wears. I approach him when he is sitting on the bench, legs open, and find any excuse to engage him in conversation.

How was your weekend, Mr Mitchell?

Can't believe it's still snowing, eh, Mr Mitchell?

Are you going to supervise the school dance, Mr Mitchell?

He always responds with a cocky ease, and I smile and nod, waiting for him to blink or look away after the socially appropriate amount of eye contact has ended, so that I can steal a peek up his shorts, an image I will summon later that night.

On the day he catches me peeking, he is wearing boxers with little dogs on them.

# MOUSTACHE

My body is disappearing. Armpits, chest, belly button, arms, fingers, legs, and toes that were once bare are now lost somewhere under multiplying hair. There is even hair down there. My brother and I try to compare our hair-growths at dinner, but my parents tell us this is inappropriate to share. We must grow hairy alone. Thankfully, most of the hairs are hidden. Just not the ones rising above my lips.

Nice moustache! I know it's not a compliment. I ask my parents if I can shave. You aren't old enough. A year of family birthday photographs all feature my newest facial highlight, joining forces with the splatter of acne and the oversize purple tortoise-shell glasses. I ask my parents if I can shave again. Don't be like one of these Canadian children always in a rush to grow up! My moustache becomes my trademark.

When I am fifteen, my parents are ready to make a compromise. They tell me to shower and come to the living room. I dash down the staircase to find my mom holding a silver tray with an oil lamp, a twenty-dollar bill, and something small wrapped in newspaper. She waves the flame around my face, blessing me and removing any mark made by evil spirits. She tells me, You are a man now, and hands me the money and the present. I rip open the wrapping to find a new shiny pair of small scissors. I am allowed to trim my moustache. I can't wait to try them out.

My trimmed moustache looks like ground black pepper glued above my lips.

I have a stolen fantasy of what my first shave will be like. My dad and I are facing the washroom mirror. We have matching white towels around our waists, and our faces are covered in white foam. Our razors are laid out in front of us. He picks his up, shaves a small strip of his cheek, rinses the blade under the tap, and then faces me for my turn, watching to make sure I don't accidentally cut myself. I pick up my brand-new razor, fighting the nerves in my hand, and try to re-enact exactly what he has done, looking at him all the while from the corner of my eye. We repeat this ritual until our faces are smooth and hurt from smiling.

My dad tells me how to shave over dinner.

Can you show me?

No, it's easy.

# GIRLS GET PREGNANT

Lately she has actually been speaking to me! Perhaps she has noted my incredible sense of style, which mostly consists of copying her style—Club Monaco sweatshirt inside-out—or the TLC poster in my locker. Maybe she is finally responding to the friend charm I put on her at the beginning of the year. She will be mine. But it's Grade Eight, and no one questions when they are chosen. Especially when they are chosen by Vicky Macker and her portal into the land of the Cool

Kids. I let her write song lyrics on my neon green plastic pencil kit with Wite-Out, and together we earnestly sing Sheryl Crow and sigh.

Vicky Macker has dyed her hair red. This added colour radiates from her like she is a new sun, her already bright personality now on fire. I am awestruck.

Wow, Vicky! Your hair looks soo good!

Thanks!

I wish I could dye my hair ...

Oh my god, we should totally dye your hair!

Really!? What colour?

Red! Just like mine!

My hair is black, it won't work.

You just need the right kind of hair dye. Like with bleach. Come over and I will do it for you! It will be so much fun!

This is my induction, my own episode of My So-Called Life. I am the Angela Chase to her Rayanne Graff.

Mom? Dad? Can I go to Vicky Macker's house this weekend?

Vicky Macker? Why do you want to go to her house? We have never met her parents.

She is going to dye my hair ...

Colour your hair??! Why would you want to colour your beautiful jet-black hair? These people would die for our hair!

I just want to see what it would look like ...if it was red ...

RED? No! The next thing you know Vicky Macker will get pregnant and we can't afford any alimony.

# SUNDAYS

After a week of pop quizzes and knives in your back, the weekend is a universal sanctuary. TGIF! But while my classmates have plans of testing out their new fake IDs or hooking up with their best friend's almost ex-boyfriend, I have been eagerly anticipating something altogether different. Sunday.

No matter what has happened during the week or what I have been called, I am only a few days away from Sunday.

*I am only a few days away from Sunday.*

On Sundays, believers come together to pray at the Centre, mostly in the form of *bhajans*, Sanskrit Hindu songs. I pester my parents to drive me there two hours before the prayers begin. When I walk in, I am greeted with familiar sandalwood incense, classical Indian flute playing in the distance, and a large elephant-headed gold statue. I smile and say *Sai Ram* to the other followers who are all wearing white, head to toe, just like me. No one is an outsider here.

I stride into the main hall and commence my sadhana. I spread white sheets on the carpet and place rose petals on the holy pathway, each petal an offering from my heart. On the altar stage, I carefully remove last Sunday's dying flower garlands from the life-sized pictures and make sure there is enough oil in the lamps. I don't sit down until I am sure the space is perfect. I turn around, and the entire hall, which used to be an old theatre for adult films, is full. The prayers commence with an enormous AUM, and my entire body shakes.

When it's my turn to sing, my heart brims with love, and I consciously, tangibly pour that love into every syllable. *Tere siva prabhu koi nahi hey tujako mera pranam.* I sing loud and full. I want God to hear me. I want the congregation to hear me too. And they do. After the service, when they come to talk to me, I look for the question mark on their foreheads or in their eyes, the one I have grown accustomed to seeing from Mondays to Saturdays, the one that asks various incarnations of: *What's wrong with you?*

Their lips part and it sounds to me like a *bhajan*, just a different kind. This one is dedicated to me and translates to: *We love you! We approve! We wish our children could be just like you!*

I store these melodies and play them on repeat all through the week.

# GOD LIVES IN INDIA

When man is bad, God comes to Earth in a human body to bring change. This is what I learn in Sunday school. I learn that man has been bad and God, as promised, has come. God lives in India. His name is Sai Baba, which means Divine Mother and Father. I learn that Baba has come to remind everyone that they too are God, but they have just forgotten.

I understand that I am supposed to be focusing somehow on remembering my own god ways, but it is so much easier to love His. I wear His face around my neck. I plaster my bedroom walls with His photos, transforming it into an enchanted altar, candles included. He is my rock 'n' roll God, with an Afro to match. I stare at Him for hours. *Can you see me?* I memorize every name, learn every song, chant every prayer I can find to bring us closer. To bind us. God is my first love.

I tie a red ribbon around a tree in the field to mark it, render it holy, and I meditate at its foot during recess. I climb the playground hill to speak to Him. I name it Mount Sinai. I speak to Him everywhere, all the time. I ask Him to create a force field around our house to protect my family and me from being kidnapped. I ask Him to make sure I die before my parents and to manifest at my funeral and lift me to the skies. I conjure rain to prove His love for me—*Brahma let it rain, Vishnu let it rain*—and it pours. In my dreams, I am in a crowd waiting for Him. He walks right to me. We sit together, and He tells me things that I won't remember in the morning. But having Him actually visit me in my dream confirms our bond. God is my first best friend.

When we visit Baba in India for the first time, I am ten years old. We drive under giant arches adorned by angels into the ashram. They sing to me: Welcome home. I get out of the car and kiss the gravel. We line up silently with thousands of others, all dressed in white, and wait in front of His home. It is a grand mixture of mandir meets mansion, painted pastel blue yellow, and pink like all the other buildings in the ashram, complete with the necessary domes, Hindu-inspired carvings, and glittering chandeliers. Hours pass cross-legged until soft sitar sounds emerge from hidden speakers. All I can hear is my heart. There is a collective gasp and focus at the front. I see orange. It is Him! God in the flesh! He moves gracefully, gliding across the sand, His big hair swirling in the dry breeze. I commit my eyes to Him, absorbing His every gentle gesture and turn. I never want to leave. I am leaving half of my soul here in Your care and will return for it when we can be together.

At twelve, I tell my parents that they are just my earth parents, just as Baba told His at thirteen. I want to live in India with my true parent. He is calling me. I tell them I will study in His school. But the only way to get into Baba's school is for Him to accept you in person. My parents agree to grant me my four-month summer holiday to acquire His permission.

My dad and I fly to India, and after his month of vacation days expires, he leaves me in the care of a mother who is also trying to get her children into His school. Baba will watch over you.

Every day I take a copy of my application form and wait for Him in the sweltering south-Indian heat, feet blistered, hoping He will pass by me. Do you remember me? Silence. I examine the blessed others, the ones beside me or behind me that Baba graces, speaks to, chooses, determined to uncover the pattern behind His attention. Who does God love? Maybe if I was white, maybe if I was a girl, maybe if I was younger, maybe if I was older, maybe if I was prettier, maybe if I was troubled, maybe if I was kinder, maybe if I fasted, maybe if I recite the Gayathri mantra 108 times, maybe if I didn't lie to the woman selling flowers yesterday. The other followers feel sorry for me and tell me He is just testing my faith. So I remain hopeful and bend as best I can to fit the newest criteria that my sleuthing has led me to, certain of success each time. He doesn't take notice. Don't you remember me?

Summer is over. I return to Canada. God is my first broken heart.

# DIRTY THOUGHTS

I had been warned about Rajesh. The students had said, He's weird. Those words are familiar. I take it upon myself to prove them wrong, to be extra nice to him, saving him a seat next to me in the cafeteria or lending him my favourite book. We are all brothers and sisters, after all, at least in the ashram.

One afternoon, a couple hours before Baba emerges for evening bhajans, I am exploring the compound, taking advantage of the rare cool air in the midst of the sleepless heat. I hear a familiar voice say Sai Ram. I turn around. It's Rajesh. I give him a big smile. Sai Ram, Rajesh. I wonder if I should call him Uncle Rajesh, which is the polite thing to do when speaking to elders. He asks if he can join me, and I am thankful for the company. I haven't seen my family in two months, and aside from the students in Baba's school who occasionally talk to me, mistaking me for a fellow student, I keep to myself. He tells me about his many visits to the ashram and the blessings he and his family have received from Baba over the years, confirming for me his goodness. He's not weird, he's just from a different generation.

He tells me there is a beautiful garden up ahead that I have to see. I remember my mom telling me how majestic the gardens in India are. Perhaps it will be somewhere I can meditate. We walk further and further away from the ashram. I notice the change in the colour of the sky and remember time.

How far is it?

We are almost there ... Do you ever hcve dirty thoughts?

What do you mean?

Do you ever have dirty thoughts?

About?

You know ... Dirty Thoughts?

Maybe we should head back.

Don't worry. We're almost there.

Would it be all right if you showed me another time? I don't want to miss a chance to give Baba the letter I wrote.

Don't feel bad if you have dirty thoughts. Just pray.

I turn around and start walking back towards the ashram. Maybe they were right. He doesn't say anything but continues to walk beside me. I notice that aside from the piles of dirt and dried-out trees, we are alone. I walk a little faster but keep a half smile on my face, only slowing down when the pink and blue ashram gates are visible. Then I remember my letter.

I forgot something in my room. I should go get it. Thank you for sharing your stories with me. See you around?

I can come with you ...

No, it's okay. I will be fine. You should line up so you can get a good view.

I dart off in the direction of the apartment. He is still walking beside me. When we get there, I tell him I am going to run in and will be out in a second. But he follows me into my small room, which seems to have shrunk since I left it this morning. He sits on my bed. I quickly look for the letter. I am sweating.

I found it! Let's go.

Why don't you sit next to me ...

We should go.

Do you not like me?

I like you, I just don't want to miss the evening bhajans.

Just sit next to me for a second.

I look at him on the bed, sad and hunched over, like the last one to get picked for a team. I know that feeling. He is my brother, I tell myself. I sit down next to him. He lifts his leg and rests it on mine.

Are you having dirty thoughts?

I try to push his leg off so I can stand up. It's heavy and anchored down. He grabs my face with his hands and slams his chapped lips against mine. I close my eyes and hold my breath. I pray. He lets go.

Did you have dirty thoughts?

I gasp for air and disappear. I watch as my body quietly lifts off the bed. Leaves the room. Locks the door. Walks back to the ashram. He walks slightly behind me. *See you around?* he says. *Sai Ram,* I whisper.

The letter is still on the bed.

When the *bhajans* rise and Baba appears, I fight over the heads in front of me to make eye contact. *Where were You this afternoon? Were You testing me? Am I different now?* Like spoiled milk.

I was warned. And I had dirty thoughts.

# SUICIDE JEANS

When it snows, God is telling me: Stay at home, stay in bed, stay warm.

It snows a lot.

Not just outside, but inside my bedroom too. Except inside there are no distinct seasons. It can snow anytime. I am kind of used to it now. Sometimes it's even pretty, when it covers my entire head and makes all the thinking slow down. But not when it piles and piles up until I can't get to my closet or get through my door.

On those days, I dig a tunnel to my ghetto blaster and lie on the cold floor. I put on songs by women with big voices and broken hearts and just listen. Or sing along softly, cry along softly.

My mom can see the snow in my room. She is the only one who can, because snow follows her too. She tries so hard to melt mine with warm plates of idli and sambar soaked in ghee, but even a full belly can't stop the snow. She tells me to pray, so I do. I pray for sleep without a morning, dreams without mirrors, and pointing fingers. I pray so hard that I think the glass that protects His pictures will break. I am disappointed when it doesn't.

Sometimes she calls my name and can't hear me respond or I can't hear her, our voices frozen and suspended in the dense air. She even tries to look for me, but all she sees is snow. This is when her words pierce: *You are going to end up just like your uncles.*

This is comforting because both of my uncles are the most loved in their respective families. But still I ask: *Where did my uncles end up?*

Suicide is in your jeans.

I look down at my one pair of blue jeans. There was certainly something special about them. Ever since I put them on, people at school would say hi to me, even ask me to join them at lunchtime. Was this why?

I put my hands in my pockets. Dried-up Kleenex and a Dubble Bubble gum wrapper. Maybe suicide is very tiny, hiding under the stitching or the Bugle Boy patches placed there by the tailor as a secret prize for the owner. Maybe it can take different shapes; maybe the button is suicide.

After my mom's revelation, I start wearing my jeans more often, and whenever something really good happens, like when my parents increase my allowance or when I find out that I got the role of Lumière in the school production of *Beauty and the Beast*, I rub my hands on my thighs in excitement and gratitude. It even snows less in my bedroom when I am wearing them, and when I close my eyes I can imagine what it will feel like in a couple months to be on my bike, helmet-free and pedalling really fast under a sun that will try to stay up as late as me.

One afternoon, my jeans and I head to Social Studies class to find everyone gathered around a sobbing Marnie Jeffreys. I whisper to Larissa: *What happened?*

*Her cousin killed himself,* she whispers back.

What?

He committed suicide!

I rub my hands on my legs but don't feel the friendly, familiar rough fabric. I feel the soft and bristly disappointment of my own skin. I close my eyes instead of looking down to make sure my jeans are actually still on. I can see my bedroom, and it is snowing again.

When the bell rings, I wait for everyone to leave the classroom. I run out the side exit of the school and keeping running until I am home.

The reflection in the giant mirror in our washroom says that my jeans are still on. I stare at them for a long time, wondering how I could dislike something that I loved so much just a few hours ago, something that made me feel like there was no final exam I could fail. How could I resent an extension of my body—a newly grown extra layer of flesh that I now couldn't imagine living without? But thinking of Marnie's cousin and my mom's prediction, it feels as though the jeans and I are in a silent battle, me versus them, and I want to win.

I think of taking the jeans off and putting them in the garbage before my parents get home or throwing them into the fireplace we never turn on, but I am distracted by an unexpected sound from upstairs. Normally I would call my mom at work, but not today. I am still wearing my jeans.

I slowly climb up the stairs to my bedroom. The entrance is almost completely blocked by snow. I scrape my way to the top of the heap, crawl into my room, and manage to stand up when something hits my back. I slide to the ground and land on my face. Something turns me over.

*Are you okay?! I am so sorry, I didn't mean to throw so hard!*

Wh...aa ...?

The snowball! I am sorry!

I hear another voice.

Is he okay?

I don't know!
I'm okay...but who are you?! And *you*?! How did *you* get here?!

Slowly, buddy, take it slow. First, let's get you on your feet.

Out of the white, two brown figures gradually come into view. Two men who look like they could be my older cousins. I have never met them before. They have my dad's eyes. My body softens. They help me up.

*Are you okay?*

*Yeah, I think so ... but you might not be!*

I quickly reach for some snow, squeeze it into a ball in my fist, and throw it at the man who struck me down. We all laugh. Hours pass like this, us chasing each other in the snow. We build a tall fort in the corner between the foot of my bed and the wall. We make snow angels and snowmen until all the snow is used up.

# EYEBROWS

I learn a lot about how to be a boy from my brother and the lessons he learns in school. Not in the classroom but in the gym change room. Lessons I miss because I change in the corner, facing the teal-tiled wall, so that no one can accuse me of a wandering eye. I listen intently as he tells me how the boys discuss the pros and cons of shaving their pubic hair and other regions of their body. Girls don't like hairy. He even purchases his own trimmer. I hear a sharp buzzing coming from the washroom as he mows down his legs and chest.

But I am in no hurry to follow his lead. No one is going to see me naked anytime soon. I am more preoccupied with eyebrows.

I've watched my mother pluck her eyebrows hundreds of times. Whenever she is in the washroom, she is armed with tweezers and concentrating on her reflection. Once she spots where to strike, her hand lifts mechanically, tweezers tighten, and she precisely pulls the bad hair from its root. Her mind is somewhere far away. She is calm, comforted that there are things, however small, that can be removed, that can be changed. When she is summoned back by the sound of the garage door opening or remembers that she has to drive my brother to basketball practice, she puts down the tweezers and pencils thin almond-brown arches over the surviving hairs.

My own eyebrows look like a variation of Bert's from Sesame Street, two furry caterpillars forever headlining my face. So I pluck. And pluck. It's hard to stop. My face is changing, my eyes seem to be getting bigger and brighter, my face narrower. People say tweezing hurts, but I like the pain. Like when you floss your teeth for the first time in three weeks. I try to reciprocate with my brother, imparting to him my new lessor. He is surprisingly dubious.

When my mom tires of me constantly borrowing hers, we head down to Zellers where she buys my first pair of tweezers. She splurges on the fancy gold-plated ones. She hands them to me in the parking lot. Thanks, Mom. This passing of the torch has to be a sign. A sign that she knows my secret and loves me just the same.

# GOD IS HALF MAN HALF WOMAN

Lord Rama is banished to the forest for fourteen years by his wicked stepmother. She wants to ensure that her own son will be crowned and rule as King of Ayodhya. This is where the *Ramayana*, one of Hinduism's central texts, really begins.

Sita, daughter of the Earth and wife of Rama, dutifully follows her husband into the wild, tending to all of his needs, only to be kidnapped by the evil ten-headed demon Ravana. She is imprisoned in Ravana's garden for years until eventually being rescued by Rama and his army of monkey soldiers. Before returning to his embrace, however, she must walk through fire, to prove her chastity. She emerges pure, and together they happily return to Ayodhya where they assume their rightful throne.

But as time passes, there are whispers of doubt in the town. If my wife was in another man's kingdom for that long, I wouldn't take her back. Sita is banished to the forest again, but this time by Rama himself, who is only doing what is best for his kingdom. The people must not doubt the purity of their sovereign. Rama is the Righteous Ruler and Sita the exile, giving birth to their twins in the forest.

Fast-forward thousands of years later, and my mother is in the kitchen. She has just come home after her nine-to-five and has fed us our roti and dhal. Next, she stuffs hash browns into sandwiches for tomorrow's lunch, paper napkins with personal mom doodles included, and arranges our breakfasts on the table for the morning. Mini-Wheats in the bowls, multivitamins on the spoons. My dad isn't at home, he's at work. Or he's asleep, and the house is quiet to avoid disturbing him. Dad needs his rest. If his clock somehow synchronizes with ours, and he ends up at home and awake for dinner, he rests his hand on his head for the duration, bearing the brunt of the world, and I wonder why we make him so sad. Should he laugh in these few precious moments we have together, it is like the first glimpse of sun after a Canadian winter. If she cries because we haven't taken the garbage out or because he has bought her another present that she will have to pay for, we all know how to tune her out. So she learns to scream.

It's not until I am a little older that I find a new story. At a street-side vendor's stall in India, as I am flipping through the stack of familiar pictures of Hindu gods, I freeze at an image I have never seen. It is of a deity composed of Lord Shiva's left side and his female consort Parvati's right side. Ardhanarageeshwara.

All the lines that divide what men and women should be and should do begin to blur in the light of this explicit fusion of two gods and two sexes. I inhale deeply and exhale completely. It is as though I have found an old picture of myself or the answer to a question that I didn't have the words to ask. I bring it home with me and tape it to my bedroom door as a declaration.

I am not invisible anymore.

This book wouldn't be possible without my mom, Shemeena, Juliana, Katherine, Maureen, Kathryn, Marilyn, and Michelle. A special thank you to Arsenal Pulp Press, Cherie Dimaline, Trisha Yeo, Margot Francis, Tegan and Sara, Farzana Doctor, Brian Francis, Amber Dawn, Hannah Dyer, Natalie Kouri-Towe, Nat Hurley, Nigel Wynne and Adam Holman.

**VIVEK SHRAYA** is an artist whose body of work crosses the boundaries of music, literature, visual art, theatre, and film. God Loves Hair is her first book.

@vivekshraya / vivekshraya.com

ALSO BY VIVEK SHRAYA

The Boy & the Bindi
Death Threat
even this page is white
I'm Afraid of Men
She of the Mountains
The Subtweet
What I LOVE about being QUEER